MICRO FICTION

MICRO FICTION

An Anthology of *Really* Short Stories

EDITED BY JEROME STERN

W. W. Norton & Company
New York   London

The text of this book is composed in Adobe Garamond
with the display set in Univers Extra Black Extended
Composition by Crane Typesetting Service, Inc.
Manufacturing by Quebecor Printing, Fairfield.
Book design by Beth Tondreau Design / Robin Bentz

LIBRARY OF CONGRESS CATALOGING-IN-PUBLICATION DATA
   Micro fiction : an anthology of really short stories /
edited by Jerome Stern.
        p.   cm.
     ISBN 0-393-03968-4.—ISBN 0-393-31432-4 (pbk.)
   1. Short stories.   I. Stern, Jerome (Jerome H.)
   PN6120.2.M48   1996
   808.83'1—dc20   95-47592

W. W. Norton & Company, Inc.
500 Fifth Avenue, New York, N.Y. 10110
www.wwnorton.com

W. W. Norton & Company Ltd.
Castle House, 75/76 Wells Street, London W1T 3QT

15 16

For Jesse Lee Kercheval

Contents

Introduction

A short time ago I got a phone call from a man in New York who saw the announcement of Florida State University's World's Best Short Short Story contest. He said, "It said 250 words maximum. What is that? A misprint? I thought maybe it should read 2500 words. 2500 words is pretty short."

"No," I said. "250 words is right. It's a challenge, a problem in narrative. And it seems to be working out.

We've been running the contest since 1986, and every year we get thousands of entries."

"Oh, well, thanks." I could hear the grumble in his voice. I didn't blame him, really. This is a strange little form, demanding fictional strategies that are both ancient and yet to be discovered. Trying to write a serious piece of fiction in under 250 words sounds at first like being asked to perform a particularly perverse experiment, like being asked to paint a landscape on a grain of rice. But there are very old stories of enormous power that can only be called short shorts. Earlier than written language, there was the anecdote, the brief telling of an adventure on the hunt, a narrow escape, or a piece of good fortune.

Jokes are another traditional form of very short story. And perhaps the least understood. Their significance is deep. They are a way of expressing fears and anxieties, allowing people to relieve tensions they hardly know they have. Equally ancient are the brief animal stories. In the sixth century B.C., Aesop wrote down the collection of fables that other people have modified, elaborated, poetized, and satirized ever since. Parables are also short short stories, often with double meanings. How ancient they are is also impossible to know, but they appear in the

Old Testament, and those in the New Testament, such as the parable of the prodigal son (Luke 15:11–22), the good Samaritan (Luke 10:30–35), and the ten bridesmaids (Matthew 25:1–12), are among the most famous stories in all literature.

So the short short story is an ancient and honorable form, deeply rooted in the human psyche and in the history of human communities. But fiction has evolved as a secular art form. In the nineteenth century, the artistic possibilities of the short story began to be explored consciously. Within decades, the short story developed techniques for vividly suggesting depths of meaning. The texture of a relationship could be implied by a single observation, the life of a character by a telling gesture. From Poe, Chekhov, Gogol, Maupassant, the short story evolved to Franz Kafka, Ernest Hemingway, Katherine Anne Porter, Flannery O'Connor, and Donald Barthelme. The possibility for control, the concentration of effect, the elegance of its shape, the fluidity of its possibilities allowed the short story to become an art genre with its own evolving aesthetic.

Meanwhile the very short short story remained in the fabric of ordinary communication. Before the days of television, popular magazines regularly used to publish fiction, and the short short existed as a sort of trick form, a quick little story with an unexpected twist—something to read while you waited for your turn at the barbershop. All part of the unrecognized literature of everyday life.

So the short short story is not exactly a novelty, or a form that is entirely experimental. Nor is it an artificially constricted orifice through which the writer is asked to squeeze. In the 1960s, writers like Russell Edson and Enrique Anderson Imbert started writing stories only a few lines long, as if to pose the question "Can a short story be too short to be a short story?" College students were made aware of the question by Jack David and Jon Redfern's collection *Short Short Stories* in 1981. In 1982, Irving Howe and Ilana Weiner Howe assembled *Short Shorts: An Anthology of the Shortest Stories*. They are by some of the greatest of writers—Tolstoy, Maupassant, Hemingway—but they are at the least several pages long. Robert Shapard and James Thomas collected stories [*in Sudden Fiction, Sudden Fiction International*, and *Sudden Fiction (Continued)*], whose maximum length was five pages. In *Flash Fiction*, James Thomas, Denise Thomas, and Tom Hazuka limited their selections to three pages.

The World's Best Short Short Story Contest was invented as a hyperbolic query in the form of a competition. The hyperbole is in the limitation of 250 words, derived not perversely or arbitrarily, but from the notion of an author's most familiar unit of measure, the single typewritten page. What can be done on a single typed page in this oldest of ways of telling? What bright shapes can it contain? What are the possibilities? We asked writers to try, and promised the winner a hundred dollars and a crate of Florida oranges.

After ten years, it seemed time to expand the challenge beyond the confines of the contest. Writers all over the country were invited to take up the challenge, and many, talented and brave, responded. Out of pity, we loosened the requirements to 300 words. Their work, plus the winners and a selection of finalists from the World's Best Short Short Story Contest, make up *Micro Fiction*. These short short stories represent work by writers who have found ways to play upon a very small field, and yet to invent their own imaginative and resonant worlds.

Jerome Stern
Tallahassee

Acknowledgments

I would like to thank Allen Woodman and Hunt Hawkins for their role in the invention of the World's Best Short Short Story Contest. Thanks are due as well to the English Department of Florida State University for its support; to my colleagues in the writing program, Janet, Sheila, Virgil, and David; and to all the readers over the years who have been so diligent, perceptive, and dedicated. Special thanks to my graduate assistants who helped so unstintingly with the contest, to Delia and all those who so kindly suggested stories for inclusion in the book, and to the editors and staff of *Sundog*. I'd also like to express my gratitude to Carol Houck Smith, my editor at Norton, for her support, encouragement, and friendship.

MICRO FICTION

The Poet's Husband

Molly Giles

He sits in the front row, large, a large man with large hands and large ears, dry lips, fresh-cut hair, pink skin, clear eyes that don't blink, a nice man, calm, that's the impression he gives, a quiet man who knows how to listen; he is listening now as she sways on the stage in a short black dress and reads one poem about the time she slit her wrists and another poem about a man she still sees and a third poem about a cruel thing he himself said to her six years ago that she never forgot and never understood, and he knows that when she is finished everyone will clap and a few, mostly women, will come up and kiss her, and she will drink far too much wine, far too quickly, and all the way home she will ask, "What did you think, what did you really think?" and he will say, "I think it went very well"—which is, in fact, what he does think—but later that night, when she is asleep, he will lie in their bed and stare at the moon through a spot on the glass that she missed.

The Cough

Harry Humes

1 9 9 3   W I N N E R

Our young father walked Ash Alley whistling "Rescue the Perishing," but already he carried mine tunnels home in his black-streaked breath. It was like first sleet against an attic window. My mother would look at him, her lips a line of impatience and fear. "Your lungs will soon be stone," she said. "It's good money, Dorse. It's our only money."

Some of the men who stopped at our house to see my father had tongues like fish that stuck out between words. Gray-faced, shoulders bony, they all seemed about to cave in. My mother would leave the room, her lips thinner than ever, but the cough followed her across the linoleum, down cellar steps, hunkered close when she planted sage and primrose. The cough was like a child. It was always hungry. It demanded attention. It woke us up at odd times and sat in the good chair by the window. In the winter, it trailed behind my father like a peacock feather on a woman's hat.

One summer he told us we were on a planet going nowhere fast. He made a model he called an orrery, and showed us how the heavens worked. The center was bright and hung there like one of my mother's peony blossoms. "That there's what pushes it," he said. "And that's what made the coal."

We looked at him and nodded, but we had our own ideas about what made it go. We could hear it behind the least little thing.

Daydream

Roberta Allen

My half sister is shrieking in the front seat of the car while her husband—a gambler like our father—races through the mountains at top speed. This trip feels like a roller-coaster ride. My half sister's husband can't wait to reach Las Vegas and lose his wife's money. Their son and daughter hold each other tight in the backseat where I sit too. My half sister's daughter—who is older than me!—is also shrieking. I keep my nose pressed against the window glass. I am not afraid.

My half sister's husband laughs gleefully as he makes a hairpin turn on the steep mountain road without slowing down or honking the horn first. As we round each bend, my half sister lets out a scream and begs him to slow down. The more she pleads, the wilder he drives. "You'll kill us all!" she cries. But her husband is having too much fun to listen. I don't listen either. I don't let anyone disturb my daydream: I am home in New York with this French boy named Jean. We are rowing on the lake in Central Park. We are having a very good time.

Wrong Channel

Roberto Fernandez

Barbarita waited impatiently for her ride as beads of
sweat dripped from her eyebrows into her third cup
of cold syrupy espresso. She was headed for the toilet
when she heard the knocking sounds of Mima's old
Impala. "About time you got here," yelled Barbarita from
the Florida room.

"It wouldn't start this morning."

Barbarita got in, tilted the rearview mirror, and applied
enough rouge to her face for a healthier look. She wanted
to make a good impression on the doctor who would ap-
prove her medical records for her green card. On the way to
Jackson Memorial, Mima talked about her grandchildren.

Barbarita knocked down all the Bibles and *Reader's Digests* on the table when the nurse finally called her name.

"Sorry, ma'am, but you can't come in," the nurse said to Mima.

"I'm her interpreter," replied the polyglot.

"No bueno," said the doctor grimly as he walked in with Barbarita's X-rays. He told Mima, "Ask her if she had TB."

Mima turned to Barbarita. "He says, if you have a television?"

"Tell him yes, but in Havana. Not in Miami. But my daughter has a television here."

Mima told the doctor, "She says she had TV in Cuba, not in Miami, but her daughter has TV here."

"In that case we need to test her daughter for TB too."

Mima translated, "He says he needs to test your daughter's television to make sure it works, otherwise you cannot get your green card."

"Why the television?" asked a puzzled Barbarita.

"How many times did I tell you you needed to buy one? Don't you know, Barbarita? This is America."

Harmony

Joy Williams

June brought a friend when she went to visit her mother, who was dying. Her friend had never even met her mother, she just happened to be in town. June felt despicable, but she was terrified. She and her friend sat meekly beside her mother's bed. June picked up a book in which her mother had written with a red pen *untrue*. June thought this was dear, even catastrophic, because it was just a book of poems. Finally her friend left. Go, go, thought June carelessly. Day surrendered to night as it does, and June had the odd thought that she had never been born. The thought appeared quite gracefully and didn't seem at all inappropriate. After some time, she was aware of a fly in the room, shuffling along the window sash. She remembered her mother once saying as she had put supper on the table when June was just a child—a fresh, hot supper as was often the case—"How did that fly get in here?" It had been another fly surely, that one.

20/20

Linda Brewer

By the time they reached Indiana, Bill realized that Ruthie, his driving companion, was incapable of theoretical debate. She drove okay, she went halves on gas, etc., but she refused to argue. She didn't seem to know how. Bill was used to East Coast women who disputed everything he said, every step of the way. Ruthie stuck to simple observation, like "Look, cows." He chalked it up to the fact that she was from rural Ohio and thrilled to death to be anywhere else.

She didn't mind driving into the setting sun. The third evening out, Bill rested his eyes while she cruised along making the occasional announcement.

"Indian paintbrush. A golden eagle."

Miles later he frowned. There was no Indian paintbrush, that he knew of, near Chicago.

The next evening, driving, Ruthie said, "I never thought I'd see a Bigfoot in real life." Bill turned and looked at the side of the road streaming innocently out behind them. Two red spots winked back—reflectors nailed to a tree stump.

"Ruthie, I'll drive," he said. She stopped the car and they changed places in the light of the evening star.

"I'm so glad I got to come with you," Ruthie said. Her eyes were big, blue, and capable of seeing wonderful sights. A white buffalo near Fargo. A UFO above Twin Falls. A handsome genius in the person of Bill himself. This last vision came to her in Spokane and Bill decided to let it ride.

Your Fears Are Justified

Rick DeMarinis

There's a bomb on this plane. I offer no proof. And yet I know. Panic constricts my breathing. My heart can be heard, I'm sure of that. It ticks in my ear like an egg timer. I get out of my seat slowly so as not to alarm the others. In the rest room I splash my face with cold water. The bomb is with the cargo. We're approaching Clinic City. The plane touches down. The bomb, though armed, does not explode.

In the Clinic City hospital I have to share a room

with a heart patient. "What are you here for?" he asks. "Brain tumor," I say. He perks up, interested. "How's your ticker?" he says. His wife, large and phlegmatic, visits twice a day. They whisper. "You're terminal?" she asks, coyly. It's as if she's asked me about the weather in Des Moines. "Not that I know of," I say. "Brain tumor," her husband whispers, nudging her. They exchange loving glances. I know what they are thinking. It's clear: *They want my heart.* "Macroadenoma," I say. "Nonmalignant." They wink at each other. She consoles me with a ladyfinger. After the operation I fly home, weak but still sensitive to threats.

I appreciate your interest. I honor your adrenalized stare. Your fears are justified. I'm sorry. I will sit here in my living room and decide what to tell you. Yes, there is no hope. But remember, some fuses are duds, some tumors are benign, some heart patients recover on their own. You have time to change your life.

At the Point

Beauvais McCaddon

Darlene and Johnny ran over their Chinese pug Sugar on New Year's Eve. Although the dog lived, Darlene took it as a sign to quit drinking, and she did. Johnny said he'd cut back.

Needing a change, they moved to a weathered gray cottage with a sixty-foot tower, overlooking the ocean at Alligator Point. Darlene wanted to name their house "Beside the Point." Johnny said, "That's four-plus dumb." Every morning the dogs on their street, Sam,

Gumbo, and Red the wolfdog, went along to work, riding in the back of pickup trucks. Sugar stayed home.

"Corona and lime, party time. Let that dog be a dog," Johnny said and headed for the Pride of the Point lounge. Darlene, approaching fifty, no longer felt carefree and joyous. She walked Sugar on the deserted beach. Red, the big wolfdog, stalked them.

Darlene drove to Panacea for coffee at Pete's Saltaire. Johnny's Blazer was parked at Barfield's Oyster Bar. Darlene thought she might call her house "What's the Point?"

Returning home, Darlene found the sliding glass door open. Had Johnny set Sugar free to run as fast as his little pug legs would carry him? She climbed her tower, calling, "Come back, little Sugar, come back." Darlene knew the cottage should be "After the Point." What was there After Johnny, After Sugar?

She could hear Sugar's little yip mixed with the other dogs' barks, the wolfdog's low growls, but from her high point Darlene saw only pine trees, ocean, and red hibiscus.

The Halo

Michael McFee

When Jesus was born, I thought he had a caul; but with his first cry, it began to glow. That was the halo—always in the way, poking my breast when he nursed, nicking Joseph when he'd bend to kiss the boy good night. But if we reached to take it off, somehow it wasn't there: it was a mirage, a shadow, a little golden cloud we couldn't quite touch.

Jesus could remove it, though. He'd fly it like a kite, the sun on a string. He'd skip it across the lake and it would always return. He'd even work it into his juggling routine, pieces of fruit landing on a dazzling plate, ta-dah!

Joseph was embarrassed. Maybe the halo reminded him of what he wasn't. So he built it a fine cedar box, and made Jesus take it off and lock it inside and bury it out back under the fig tree and promise not to dig it up. Joseph told him he could have it back one day, when he was a man.

And so Jesus grew up a normal boy, and everybody forgot about the halo.

But last night I dreamed that a couple of thieves dug up the box. And when they opened it, the fig tree burst into golden fruit, hundreds of sweet halos and not a snake in sight.

Mockingbird

Laurie Berry

1989 WINNER

Peter has just returned from Mexico, where his face turned the chalky pink color of Pepto-Bismol. Rachel is at that swooning stage of love, stupid with happiness at his return.

That evening they drink cold vodka and gossip about a child-laden couple they know, who rise at dawn for work and return home at seven to bathe the three-year-old, console the eight-year-old, and struggle through dinner in time to collapse in bed by ten.

"Even so they have a great house," she says. "And nice things. They make a lot of money."

Peter shakes his head and says offhandedly: "I'd rather inherit it."

They are both shocked by the statement. An island of silence bobs to the surface. Rachel swallows the last of her vodka, and with it the realization that she is in love with a man who has just traveled to a third-world nation to play tennis.

"By the way—" He looks up guiltily, making a game of it. "Promise me you'll never tell anyone I said that."

This makes her laugh, freshens her love. They laugh some more. Talk their slow way toward dinner. Spy on the remarkable albino Mexican boy playing in the yard next door. Make love with the windows open and then lie there listening to the mariachi music that pumps through her Houston barrio neighborhood.

Everything is soft, very soft. And luck abundant as johnsongrass. The mimosa trees' green canopy. And the mockingbirds, not yet vicious, waiting for the fierce end of summer.

Changing the Channel

E. Ethelbert Miller

My father and I have pillows behind our backs. The television is on but we talk without looking at each other. It is better this way, easier for my father to find words, which interrupt his breath like commercials. It is one of those strange moments when our small apartment in the Bronx is empty. My sister is on a date with a boy she can't bring home. My brother is at church lighting candles and saying prayers which will not lengthen his life. My mother is selecting lamb chops over pork in a nearby store, and the price has nothing to do with our health. Now is the time when my father has a good job in the post office and this miracle of rest is what we share while watching old movies that offer no resemblance to who we are.

Wanting to Fly

Stephen Dunning

1 9 9 0   W I N N E R

At the State Fair a man in silver tights and handlebar mustache—some name like The Great Zambini—blasts from a cannon. Driving home, Father calls me "Goosey Zamboosi" and "Flying Weenie." But later, when I spray my BVDs with Ma's birdcage paint, he paddles me good.

Again.

For my ninth birthday, Ma gives me a silver-gray T-shirt with Halley's Comet flashing across. I can fly in that shirt—arms stiff, tilting. Then Mrs. McKissup catches us on the kindergarten slide. "You boys! Let the children use it."

In two minutes Duncan and me're in Beaver's office.

"Childish," Mr. Beaver says. "Selfish." Duncan giggles. "What would you do, you're trying to run a decent school?" We both giggle.

Father uses the hairbrush.

Duncan and me nail a refrigerator carton to the Frenzels' porch roof. Duncan falls awful hard, grabbing his ankle. "It's broke," he hollers. I run for his ma. Next rain the Frenzels' roof sprinkles like a watering can.

My last beating ever.

Wallace's Carnival hires me to assemble rides—dollar a day, food, sleep anywhere I can. We head for Toledo, Willie Farley driving the ferris-wheel truck. It's Willie teaches me cannon-flying. I get pretty famous.

Then of course Father and me get along. I'm home from Cole Brothers when Father drowns, ice-fishing with Arn Bower. Before they hook him, I see his face—mouth open and lopsided, a giant perch.

Arn Bower starts keeping Ma company, and that's good. There's women wherever I fly.

Eclipsed

Robert Shuster

Anxious not to miss the coming darkness, Gavin woke early and watched Dad construct the viewers from boxes. Behind his pile of aluminum foil, cardboard, and glue, Dad said: "You see, when the moon passes in front of the sun, like this"—he held up his hairy fists before his eyes—"my head, the earth, gets dark."

The hour approached. Standing expectantly on the front lawn, their backs to the sun, they donned their viewers. Muffled by cardboard, Dad's voice sounded distant: "See the black dot? That's the moon."

Gavin watched the white and black dot converge, his moist fingers pressed against the box. Twice he glanced through the neck hole to see if his body was wilting, or his feet sinking. He imagined the darkness—moon darkness—coating his hands.

"There," came the distant voice. "Completely covered. Hell, the next time this happens, I'll be dead."

Gavin shook off the viewer. The summer grass was brown, the sky purple. He looked at the forbidden sight—the covered sun, the patched yellow eye—and tried, quickly, to imagine his father dead and himself a man, to imagine years passing as the earth spun a thousand times. Dad, darkened, stood still, his square cardboard head bent to the ground, a space creature. Gavin jammed the box on his head. He wanted the sun.

The New Year

Pamela Painter

It's late Christmas Eve at Spinelli's when Dominic presents us, the waitstaff, with his dumb idea of a bonus—Italian hams in casings so tight they glimmer like Gilda's gold lamé stockings.

At home, Gilda's waiting up for me with a surprise of her own: my stuff from the last three months is sitting on the stoop. Arms crossed, scarlet nails tapping the white satin sleeves of her robe, she says she's heard about Fiona. I balance the ham on my hip and stuff my things—

CDs, my weights, a vintage Polaroid—in garbage bags she's provided free of charge. Then I let it all drop and offer up the ham in both hands, cradling it as if it might have been our child. She doesn't want any explanations—or the ham.

Fiona belongs to Dominic, and we are a short sad story of one night's restaurant despair. But the story's out, and for sure I don't want Dominic coming after my ham. I pack up the car and head west. The ham glistens beside me in the passenger seat. Somewhere in Indiana I even give it a seat belt.

I stop to call, but Gilda hangs up every time. So I send her pictures of my trip. The Ham under the silver arch of St. Louis; The Ham at the Grand Canyon; The Ham in Las Vegas. I'm taking a picture of The Ham in the Pacific when a big wave washes it out to sea. I send the picture anyway: The Ham in the Pacific Undertow. In this picture, you can't tell which of us is missing.

Survivors

Kim Addonizio

He and his lover were down to their last few T cells and arguing over who was going to die first. He wanted to be first because he did not want to have to take care of his lover's parrot or deal with his lover's family, which would descend on their flat after the funeral, especially the father, who had been an Army major and had tried to beat his son's sexual orientation out of him with a belt on several occasions during adolescence; the mother, at least, would be kind but sorrowful, and secretly blame him, the survivor—he knew this from her letters, which his lover had read to him each week for the past seven years. He knew, too, that they all— father, mother, two older brothers—would disapprove of their flat, of the portrait of the two of them holding hands that a friend had painted and which hung over the bed, the Gay Freedom Day poster in the bathroom, all the absurd little knickknacks like the small plastic wind-up penis that hopped around on two feet; maybe, after his lover died, he would put some things away, maybe he would even take the parrot out of its cage and open the window so it could join the wild ones he'd heard of, that nested in the palm trees on Delores Street, a whole flock of bright tropical birds apparently thriving in spite of the chilly Bay Area weather—he would let it go, fly off, and he would be completely alone then; dear God, he thought, let me die first, don't let me survive him.

Anti-Cain

Virgil Suarez

When he votes next time, he will vote Republican. What kind of foreign policy president could only do so little as to merely reduce his sentence from six blows to four. The official tells him to hang in there. The first blow burns. Sends chills up his spine. That's bamboo with ridges and knobby joints. "Fuck!" Blow number two blinds him with tears. The third one he hears more than feels as it breaks open the skin. Ah, the malice of wood. And finally the last one falls, *swiish*, cutting deepest. Four blows. It's over. He hung on, which proves his innocence. Spit on all those present. It's over for you, the officials tell him. When the official comes by to check on him, he is still pissed off. No comments. The official says his hometown will have a key to the city waiting for him. Publishers want him to write the book. For a lot of money. Do the night talk shows. Fame. There's an idea he can get used to.

Painted Devils

Fred Chappell

They had withdrawn after the last repulse, but Sergeant Belot said they would be coming back before noon. "Stand your ground," he said. "Don't get cut down from behind."

I had eight rounds, and when I asked Jean-Pierre he had six. We evened up. "Thanks, my friend," he said. "It is kind of you and causes me to regret the girl I charmed away from you in New Orleans."

"What do I care? It's like you told me once. Women are painted devils."

"That was before we met these bastards," he said. "Here they come again. These are the painted devils truly."

We had to hold our fire until we could smell their raging breath, then we gave them what we had and they pulled back suddenly and the field fell silent.

After a while the sergeant allowed it was over. "They only made a last feint to show their mettle. Now they're gone. In thirty minutes we march. We'll drink cantina beer on Friday, boys." He was colorful with dust and sweat and blood, like the rest of us.

"Not you," I told Jean-Pierre. "Here's for Rosalie in New Orleans." I swung the Springfield at his belly and pulled the trigger.

He went white then red. "Good thing for you you knew the chamber was empty," he said.

But I hadn't known. I didn't even know I'd pissed myself. "I wouldn't shoot you for a woman," I said. "Painted devils, all of them. You told me so."

Honeycomb

Natalia Rachel Singer

1 9 9 2   W I N N E R

Mrs. Stick stood breathless in her kitchen stirring ruta-bagas and pigs' knuckles into a heavy stew. She was expecting Mr. Mann, who had a produce stand in the next district where every day a gang of quarreling farmers came to weigh their squash and sugar beets on the dusty scale in his pickup. Mr. Mann was lean and oily, with black bristles of hair that could paint her belly honey yellow in flat wide strokes. She wanted him to want her but she knew he liked his women meatier, with thick toenails that could click against his like castanets. Mrs. Stick hummed the score from *Oklahoma* and waited, feeling desire part her like a comb.

When the stew was ready, she skimmed off the scum and tossed it onto her mulch pile beneath the only living elm tree in the county, two paces from her baby's grave. She thought of those eyelids less yielding than a doll's, that unbearable silence, felt the old hollow ache as wind rushed up her ash-colored skirt. When she opened her eyes again there he was, as real as grain, riding across the valley, the dust fluttering behind like a cloud of worker bees. His truck kalumphed; there were mounds of squash pounding up and down just for her.

"How much does a baby weigh?" he'd ask her when she exclaimed how big they were, how perfectly whole. After their meal they'd walk to the river while the last of the sun spit honey, their clasped fingers shortening the stretch of empty fields.

Baby, Baby, Baby

François Camoin

1991   W I N N E R

"Let's taste each other's bodies now without pleasure," Martha says.

The living room is full of dogs—she has three, I have four. They have no names; we just call them all "dog" and they never fail to understand which one we mean. It's early evening and the boys from the gas company are lined up in the street outside singing a Jerry Lee Lewis medley. They've got the grand piano strapped on the back of a flatbed truck parked under the maple trees.

They sing like angels. Breathless. Great Balls of Fire. Hang Up My Rock 'n' Roll Shoes.

"Touch me here, and here," Martha says.

High School Confidential. There's a Whole Lot of Shakin' Goin' On. They're all castrati, of course, with those thin pure high voices that signify otherness and absence.

"Baby baby baby," Martha says.

"You were the one who said without pleasure."

"It came over me like a big wind," Martha apologizes.

She looks skeletal. Ribs like an anatomy lesson. God I love her, but what can I do? This morning I made fajitas and she picked out all the bits of chicken, sailed her tortillas like Frisbees to the grateful dogs. Toyed with a piece of green pepper, swallowed slivers of onion.

Tomorrow afternoon it's supposed to be Utah Power and Light doing Janis Joplin. Big women in meter-reader uniforms singing the blues. On the far side of the room, under the moiling dogs the twins are playing. One says "Mama." The other answers "Mama Mama."

An Old Story

James Kelman

She'd been going about in this depressed state for ages so I should've known something was up. But I didnt. You dont always see what's in front of your nose. I've been sitting about the house that long. You wind up in a daze. You dont see things properly, even with the weans, the weans especially. There again but she's no a wean. No now. She's a young woman. Ach, I dont want to tell this story.

But you cant say that. Obviously the story has to get told.

Mm, aye, I know what you mean.

Fine then. Mmm.

Okay, so about your story . . .

Aye.

It concerns a lassie, right? And she's in this depressed state, because of her boyfriend probably—eh?

I dont want to tell it.

But you've got to tell it. You've got to tell it. Unless . . . if it's no really a story at all.

Oh aye christ it's a story, dont worry about that.

Conception

Tom Fleming

1 9 9 5   W I N N E R

Mother had seen Father in town, squatting in the shadow of his hulking Dodge wagon, scratching his head with a car key. The light bisected him, burning into Mother's memory an elbow forever cocked, a silvery hand, a restless wispy smile. Inside they drew the curtains and made love on a bed of fresh canvas.

The rich smell still lingering in her hair, they drove to his clapboard house. As he carried her inside, he paused in the doorway to throw the Dodge's key into a nearby stand of salt tamarisk as a testament to their love.

He'll leave you, Mother's people said. *His kind pops across the desert with every storm.*

But look, Mother answered, look . . .

And when they did, there were more—the Willys Overland, the Packard Clipper. By month's end there were even more: the Model A, the Hudson pickup, the gap-toothed Plymouth, grinning through its broken grill. The keys glittered in the tamarisk. And one night a band of pack rats homesteaded there, dragging mesquite branches and the bones of animals to the site, thrilled to awe by the shine.

And when Mother saw the nest, towering over the yard like a jewel, she ran inside to wake him. An omen she cried, Look!

How they wept! I see their faces, creased with pride, and hear Mother's laugh as she led him into the yard, back to the Dodge. I imagine her voice, coaxing gravelly as an angel's, the sight of raindrops clinging to the chrome strip running down the hood, the hot feel of my approaching life on my mother's thigh.

All This

Joanne Avallon

Your arm and hand cock back instinctively, although they have never moved like this before, because your firstborn has taken a piece of your thigh between her two-year-old, sharp and white incisors, and it surprises you to find your arm in this position, you who dress her naked dolls so they won't look cold, but her teeth take deeper hold and drive everything out of your head except, oddly, your own father saying "silly bitch" when you were five and left your bike out in the rain and also the sound, so compelling, of skin hitting skin and, even more oddly, something your aunt told you about your grandfather boxing your father's ear so bad it bled rough red stuff from the eardrum—all this, even the love you feel for both these men, rushes through you so fast you understand for the first time—as your hand descends— the phrase "seeing red" and the only thing between your hand and your child is your puny intellect scared shitless in some corner, so that just before your hand hits the tender part of her thigh, the part you had kissed just twenty minutes ago when changing her diaper and before she screams, your daughter looks at you first in disbelief and then in complete comprehension, as though, perhaps, she knew these stories all along, and you wonder, with terror, as you've never wondered before, if this is the history you've been trying to write.

Stone Belly Girl

Jamie Granger

1994 WINNER

That year when the St. Kitts carnival came around, the stone belly girl had a cold. Three months before, she'd begun to bleed down there, and her aunt had explained to her all that that meant. And even though she had told her father no, not this year, she held his big calloused hand—his other grasped the hammer—as they mounted the wooden steps to the stage. Before the grandstand, the children, policemen, and steel drum band, the mothers, masqueraders, and the soft drink and Sno-Kone stands, she waited for the crowd to subside, like the sea sometimes did before it rained.

Then the stone belly girl got down on her back, sniffled, and lifted her thin cotton dress toward her narrow chest. This dress was so unlike the gowns the girls in the Miss St. Kitts Pageant wore. But she'd worn it every year since the first, when her father, loud and drunk, had pushed her into the mud behind the grandstand and busted a small flat rock on her stomach with a nailhammer. Now her father came toward her with the big rounded stone, smooth as a calabash in his hands, and lowered it gently down, sea salt glistening on its black skin, onto her brown belly. The stone belly girl wanted to blow her nose, but instead relaxed under the weight, as she had learned to do, and watched the polished hammerhead go up and come down. Once and then once more before the stone broke like an egg, the two halves rolling off her, and she stood up and coughed.

Worry

Ron Wallace

She worried about people; he worried about things. And between them, that about covered it.

"What would you think of our daughter sleeping around?" she said.

"The porch steps are rotting," he replied. "Someone's going to fall through."

They were lying in bed together, talking. They had been lying in bed together talking these twenty-five years. First about whether to have children, he wanted to (although the roof was going fast); she didn't (Down's syndrome, leukemia, microcephaly, mumps). Then, after their daughter was born, a healthy seven pounds eleven ounces ("She's not eating enough"; "The furnace is failing"), they talked about family matters, mostly ("Her friends are hoodlums, her room is a disaster"; "There's something about the brakes, the water heater's rusting out").

Worry grew between them like a son, with his own small insistencies and then more pressing demands. They stroked and coddled him; they set a place for him at the table; they sent him to kindergarten, private school, and college. Because he failed at nearly everything and always returned home, they loved him. After all, he was their son.

"I've been reading her diary. She does drugs. She sleeps around."

"I just don't think I can fix them myself. Where will we find a carpenter?"

Their daughter married her high school sweetheart, had a family, and started a health food store in a distant town. Although she recalled her childhood as fondly as anyone—how good her parents had been and how they worried for her, how old and infirm they must be growing, their house going to ruin—she rarely called or visited. She had worries of her own.

You Can't See Dogs on the Radio

Linda Wendling

The swan on still St. Mary's Lake
Float double, swan and shadow!
We will not see them; will not go,
To-day, nor yet to-morrow . . .
—*Wm. Wordsworth, "Yarrow Unvisited"*

oping to someday escape the taint of the family's mediocrity, Dad's Uncle Phil spent a year ("No trouble . . .") rearing twin dogs and parrots for the Doublemint Gum commercials on the radio. (I believe his plan included giving heave-ho to Dad's auntie—she who continuously crossed her arms over her high, severe bosom and warned, "Relying solely on parrots never got anybody anything." But all he mentioned was a lifetime income and a new radio.)

The audition was tough. Yet, there were some good moments, when the dogs rolled over—spaniels that looked and moved "like the two selves inside every man," Dad heard Uncle Phil murmur. But you can't see dogs on the radio.

The tense moment came when the parrots were to sing. But all they'd been able to master was "Double your."

"Pleasure" was too much for them, I guess, as for Auntie.

After the audition, Phil's health declined rapidly. Cardiac arrest hit while being arrested for shoplifting a pinup of the Andrews Sisters under his shirt.

After the funeral no one would take his animals.

"No personality," Dad said, "and no pleasure."

Be Yarrow stream unseen, unknown!
It must, or we shall rue it:
We have a vision of our own;
Ah! why should we undo it?

The True Story of Mr. and Mrs. Wong

Marilyn Chin

Mrs. Wong bore Mr. Wong four children, all girls. One after the other, they dropped out like purple plums. Years passed. One night after long hours at the restaurant and a bad gambling bout Mr. Wong came home drunk. He kicked the bedstead and shouted, "What do you get from a turtle's rotten womb but rotten turtle eggs?" So, in the next two years he quickly married three girls off to a missionary, a shell-shocked ex-Marine, and an anthropologist. The youngest ran away to Hollywood and became a successful sound specialist.

Mr. Wong said to Mrs. Wong, "Look what happened to my progeny. My ancestors in heaven are ashamed. I am a rich man now. All the Chinese restaurants in San Jose are named Wong. Yet, you couldn't offer me a healthy son. I must change my fate, buy myself a new woman. She must have fresh eggs, white and strong." So, Mr. Wong divorced Mrs. Wong, gave her a meager settlement, and sent her back to Hong Kong, where she lived to a ripe old age as the city's corpse beautician.

Two years ago, Mr. Wong became a born-again Christian. He now loves his new wife, whose name is Mrs. Fuller-Wong. At first she couldn't conceive. Then, the Good Lord performed a miracle and removed three large polyps from her womb. She would bear Mr. Wong three healthy sons who would all become corporate tax accountants.

Flu

Stuart Dybek

Faye's illness had transformed her in a way no diet or face-lift could have. After days of nausea, vertigo, diarrhea; a fast of toast and tea; fever; dreams that came and went more like mirages; an aching lethargy that demanded fourteen-hour sleeping spells from which she'd wake confused, but only too aware of how terribly alone she was, Faye felt better.

The usual grim weariness was gone from around her lips. Her eyes no longer peered out like a miner's from sallow tunnels smudged with mascara. They seemed enlarged with light, glowing limpidly from her pale face. Even the shadow beneath her chin, where her darkness most accumulated, had burned away. It was as if everything unessential had burned away. "What happened to you?" Aldo blurted, startled by the sight of her sitting, legs crossed, back behind the reception desk.

"Flu," Faye said. "Everybody's getting it. I mean, you sit up here in front all day and you're going to come in contact with everything anybody walks in with."

"Everybody should get so sick," Aldo said.

It seemed to Faye an odd remark at the time, but she ignored it and kept talking, about the job, the weather, the flu epidemic. It was the first conversation she'd had since she'd been sick and she clung to it, needing desperately to talk, aware the entire time of how Aldo was watching her.

And later, when people would ask them how they met and fell in love, it was always Aldo who would answer. "Flu." He'd smile earnestly. "It all started with flu. I still haven't recovered."

The Bridge

Russell Edson

In his travels he comes to a bridge made entirely of bones. Before crossing he writes a letter to his mother: Dear mother, guess what? the ape accidentally bit off one of his hands while eating a banana. Just now I am at the foot of a bone bridge. I shall be crossing it shortly. I don't know if I shall find hills and valleys made of flesh on the other side, or simply constant night, villages of sleep. The ape is scolding me for not teaching him better. I am letting him wear my pith helmet for consolation.

The bridge looks like one of those skeletal reconstructions of a huge dinosaur one sees in a museum. The ape is looking at the stump of his wrist and scolding me again. I offer him another banana and he gets very furious, as though I'd insulted him. Tomorrow we cross the bridge. I'll write to you from the other side if I can; if not, look for a sign. . . .

Kennedy in the Barrio
Judith Ortiz Cofer

My sixth-grade class had been assigned to watch the Kennedy inauguration on television and I did at the counter of Puerto Habana, the restaurant where my father worked. I heard the Cuban owner Larry Reyes say that an Irish Catholic being elected meant that someday an Hispano could be president of the United States too. I saw my father nod in automatic agreement with his boss, but his eyes were not on the grainy screen; he was mainly concerned with the food cooking in the back and with the listless waitress mopping the floor. Larry Reyes turned his attention to me then and raised his cup as if to make a toast: "Here's to a puertorriqueño or puertorriqueña president of the United States," he laughed, not kindly I thought.

"Right, Elenita?"

I shrugged my shoulders. Later my father would once again reprimand me for not showing Mr. Reyes the proper respect.

Two years and ten months later I would run to Puerto Habana on a cold Friday afternoon to find a crowd of people around the television set. Many of them, men and women both, were sobbing like children. "Dios mio, Dios mio," they kept wailing. A group of huddling women tried to embrace me as I made my way to my parents, who were holding each other tightly, apart from the others. I slipped in between them. I smelled her scent of castile soap, café con leche, and cinnamon; I inhaled his mixture of sweat and Old Spice cologne—a man-smell that I was afraid to like too much.

Grief

Ron Carlson

The King died. Long live the King. And then the Queen died. She was buried beside him. The King died and then the Queen died of grief. This was the posted report. And no one said a thing. But you can't die of grief. It can take away your appetite and keep you in your chamber, but not forever. It isn't terminal. Eventually you'll come out and want a toddy. The Queen died subsequent to the King, but not of grief. I know the royal coroner, have seen him around, a young guy with a good job.

The death rate for the royalty is so much lower than that of the general populace. The coroner was summoned by the musicians, found her on the bedroom floor, checked for a pulse, and wrote "Grief" on the form. It looked good. And it was necessary. It answered the thousand questions about the state of the nation.

He didn't examine the body, perform an autopsy. If he had, he wouldn't have found grief. "There is no place for grief in the body." He would have found a blood alcohol level of one point nine and he would have found a clot of improperly chewed tangerine in the lady's throat which she had ingested while laughing.

But this seems a fine point. The Queen is dead. Long live her grief. Long live the Duke of Reddington and the Earl of Halstar who were with me that night entertaining the Queen in her chambers. She was a vigorous sort. And long live the posted report which will always fill a royal place in this old kingdom.

Mount Olive

Monifa A. Love

ount Olive Primitive Baptist Church is two miles from my home. She is a calla lily growing in deep woods. On the third Sunday of each month, I sit in the middle of the fourth pew beneath the jade shower of the skylight. I join other ample women and our rail-thin sisters in testimony and tears. The hymns are cradles and bayonets—nesting our laments and pressing us on. We sing like we have known each other all of our lives; our voices thickly woven ropes, making ladders. Vaselined children with swinging feet draw on their legs and rock to the rhythm. Thin brown men in thinning brown suits punctuate the preacher's cadence with shouts and the percussion of their canes and polished shoes. The faithful rise and fall in the spirit like dolphin. Guardians in starched white uniforms resuscitate the overwhelmed with gentle, gloved pats to powdered faces. The elder women whisper underground words to call the faint back from their peaceful homes. They wield their fans with the skill of a signal corps. Elation evaporates from our bodies. Mercy rains down. Our tongues capture the tonic and we are saved. The service ends with hummingbirds calling "A-men" and the reverberation of small, powerful wings. We drift out to our cars. Well-worn leather bibles cross our hearts and touch the sky. The children pile into backseats to watch the church disappear through dusty windshields; their minds on early supper.

Hurray for Hollywood

George Garrett

"Couple of minutes is all, Sammy. Please?"

You call him Sammy carefully. He looks at a wrist-watch you will never be able to afford.

"Here's the thing. Big band and a couple of Fortune 500 companies create a magic credit card, the Aladdin card, unlimited, billions in credit. To be awarded by computer to one person only. Card is supposed to go to a charismatic guy who's in on the gag. But the computer goofs. Card goes to a nerd, this librarian in New Hampshire.

"The nerd doesn't believe in credit cards. Won't use it. Act One is they *make* him use it. He disappears, turns outlaw. They hire his dopey fiancée to go after him. Meantime, Act Two, everybody else wants the card—the Mafia, the FBI, the IRA, the CIA, the Democratic National Committee, I mean everybody. Cut to the chase. He's in all kinds of disguises. Ties in with a basic blond bimbo and they crisscross the country, fucken their brains out. Sharon Stone could be the bimbo. Or Kim Basinger. Act Three is how he goes bananas, buying everything including the whole state of Idaho. Now everybody wants to kill him. Even the bimbo. But just in time the fiancée catches up with him. He sees the light. Shreds the card. Marries the broad. Goes home to check out books to old ladies and horny teenagers, happily ever after. . . .

"For the nerd, I see Tom Hanks . . . maybe Tom Cruise . . . Tom Robbins?"

"It's Tim."

"Whatever. . . . Wait a minute, Sammy . . . how about Kate Moss and Johnny Depp together at last? . . . Good talking to you, Sammy, sir. . . ."

Nice watch you got there, asshole.

This Is How I Remember It

Betsy Kemper

Watching Joey pop the red berries into his mouth like Ju-Ju Bees and Mags only licking them at first, then chewing, so both of their smiles look bloody and I laugh though I don't eat even one . . . then suddenly our moms are all around us (although mine doesn't panic till she looks at the others, then screams along with them things like *God dammit did you eat these?* and shakes me so my "No" sounds like "oh-oh-oh") and then we're being yanked toward the house, me for once not resisting as my mother scoops me into her arms, and inside the moms shove medicine, thick and purple, down our throats in the bathroom; Joey in the toilet, Mags in the sink, me staring at the hair in the tub drain as my mom pushes my head down, and there is red vomit everywhere, splashing on the mirror and powder-blue rugs, everywhere except the tub where mine is coming out yellow, the color of corn muffins from lunch, not a speck of red, *I told you*, I want to scream, and then it is over and I turn to my mother for a touch or a stroke on the head like the other moms (but she has moved to the doorway and lights a cigarette, pushes hair out of her eyes) and there is only her smeared lips saying, *This will teach you anyway.*

November

Ursula Hegi

When my daughter finds me standing in the swimming pool, water up to my ribs in November, the beige of my wool dress darkened with moisture, she'll cancel her wedding. Even when she was a girl, she could be stubborn, but I always knew how to stop her. Sometimes just words—*you're making my heart ache*—and holding on to my chest. Once, when she wanted to buy that foolish motorbike, I pushed the bread knife into her hand—*you might as well slash my throat*. Now she insists on marrying. She's barely thirty-one, and I told her there's no rush, even broke my crystal glasses and stepped on them with my bare feet. But she only walked away and locked herself in her room at the end of the hall.

Arms raised straight out from my sides, I stand in the icy water, my palms inches above the cloudy surface. My legs and feet feel numb, swollen, as though they belonged to someone else, but my belly is warm. I wait for the sound of my daughter's car, the slapping of her tires against the pavement, the reassuring latch of her car door. She'll come running toward the pool and cry out my name, kneel down and offer both hands to me. . . . But it is quiet. Only the sky comes closer, the hazy dome tilting across the edges of the pool.

Carpathia

Jesse Lee Kercheval

It happened on my parents' honeymoon. The fourth morning out from New York, Mother woke to find the *Carpathia* still, engines silent. She woke Father; they rushed to the deck in their nightgowns. The first thing they saw was the white of an ocean filled with ice, then they saw white boats, in groups of two or three, pulling slowly toward the *Carpathia*. My father read the name written in red across their bows—*Titanic*. The sun was shining. Here and there a deck chair floated on the calm sea. There was nothing else.

The survivors came on board in small groups. Women and children. Two sailors for each boat. The women of the *Carpathia* went to the women of the *Titanic*, wrapping them in their long warm furs. My mother left my father's side to go to them. The women went down on their knees on the deck and prayed, holding each other's children. My father stood looking at the icy water where, if he had been on the other ship, he would be.

When the *Carpathia* dropped off the survivors in New York, my parents too got off and took the train home, not talking much, the honeymoon anything but a success. At the welcome-home party, my father got drunk. When someone asked about the *Titanic*, he said, "They should have put the men in the lifeboats. Men can marry again, have new families. What's the use of all those widows and orphans?" My mother, who was standing next to him, turned her face away. She was pregnant, eighteen. She was the one drowning. But there was no one there to rescue her.

Chickens

Elaine Magarrell

In the killing yard a man sharpens a razor, says a few words to God, and does a nice killing. After plucking and gutting he cooks the bird in a coat of its own beaten eggs. When he eats the flesh it is with pleasure. Every night he goes to bed satisfied. Every day he wakes up hungry. The chickens complain to heaven and a chicken angel is sent to earth. At first she helps the man dream about red meat so that he wakes with an appetite for steak. In a meadow he stalks a cow but is intimidated by its intrepid stare, the importance of its dung. So apprehensive is he that he goes to bed hungry.

The chickens rejoice. They have an ambassador.

That night the chicken angel sits on the man's pillow and lectures him about vegetables. At daybreak she sows for the man a garden where vegetables fairly leap from the ground. But the man finds carrots and lettuces frightening, the way they appear out of nothing. A captive of habit, he hungers for chicken.

As a last resort the chicken angel tells him how hunger cleanses the body and makes it holy. The man is intrigued by the notion of fasting. He asks God's approval and takes distant thunder for an affirmative answer.

Only so much can be done with intervention, the chicken angel reports to heaven. Having won for the chickens a respite, she leaves. Not that the chickens expected more.

The Mayor of the Sister City
Speaks to the Chamber of Commerce
in Klamath Falls, Oregon, on a
Night in December in 1976

Michael Martone

1986 WINNER

"It was after the raid on Tokyo. We children were told
to collect scraps of cloth. Anything we could find. We
picked over the countryside; we stripped the scarecrows.
I remember this remnant from my sister's obi. Red silk
suns bounced like balls. And these patches were quilted
together by the women in the prefecture. The seams were
waxed as if to make the stitches rainproof. Instead they
held air, gases, and the rags billowed out into balloons, the
heavy heads of chrysanthemums. The balloons bobbed as

the soldiers attached the bombs. And then they rose up to the high wind, so many, like planets, heading into the rising sun and America. . . ."

I had stopped translating before he reached this point. I let his words fly away. It was a luncheon meeting. I looked down at the tables. The white napkins looked like mountain peaks of a range hung with clouds. We were high above them on the stage. I am yonsei, the fourth American generation. Four is an unlucky number in Japan. The old man, the mayor, was trying to say that the world was knit together with threads we could not see, that the wind was a bridge between people. It was a hot day. I told these beat businessmen about children long ago releasing the bright balloons, how they disappeared ages and ages ago. And all of them looked up as if to catch the first sight of the balloons returning to earth, a bright scrap of joy.

Confirmation Names

Mariette Lippo

We studied the saints, slipped the boys in through a break in the hockey field's fence, and led them to the woods the nuns had deemed "off-limits."

Vicky let a boy read her palm there. He told her her lifeline was short, that she'd better learn reverence for the moment. She cried for weeks before choosing the name Barbara, patron saint of those in danger of sudden death.

Susan said she would only go "so far," but no one

knew what that meant. Boys went nuts trying to find out. They loved to untie her waist-long hair, to see it fan underneath her. She loved their love letters, the way they'd straighten up whenever she walked by. She chose Thecla, who'd caused the lions to "forget themselves"; instead of tearing her to shreds, they licked her feet.

Jackie couldn't wait for anything. The nuns told her impatience was her cross. Even the lunches her mother packed would be gone before ten, and she'd be left sorry, wanting more. She'd chosen Anthony, "the Finder," in a last-ditch effort to recover what she'd lost. But the nuns gave her Euphrasia, the virgin, who'd hauled huge rocks from place to place to rid her soul of temptation.

Before mass, we'd check her back for leaves.

None of us, of course, chose Magdalen, the whore. She was the secret patron whose spirit, we believed, watched over us from the trees. She was the woman who'd managed to turn her passion sacred. She was the saint who turned the flesh Divine.

Hostess

Amy Hempel

She swallowed Gore Vidal. Then she swallowed Donald Trump. She took a blue capsule and a gold spansule— a B-complex and an E—and put them on the tablecloth a few inches apart. She pointed the one at the other. "Martha Stewart," she said, "meet Oprah Winfrey."

She swallowed them both without water.

Housewife

Amy Hempel

She would always sleep with her husband and with another man in the course of the same day, and then the rest of the day, for whatever was left to her of that day, she would exploit by incanting, "*French* film, *French* film."

Land's End

Antonya Nelson

Her foot begins bleeding on the beach, cut by the jagged funnel of a broken bottle. *Cerveza*, she thinks, and, also, that her blood is the only thing there belonging to her. Foreign country, driven to in a friend's truck, the shirt she wears from a long-ago lover, crusty no-color shorts found folded in the house, and the house itself, ahead, that belongs to an uncle. Her bloodprints in the sand like valentines.

She's been running again, this time on foot, running

south, she's come from unlikely Kansas to the Mexican Gulf, sliding down her own country, gravitating toward the equator. At the border a toothless woman sold her a shrink-wrapped Saint Dymphna, patroness of nervous disorders. She laughed, but uneasily. Did a sane person laugh, all alone? The Mexican had three teeth, no more. Where do all the world's teeth go, she wonders now, hobbling dizzily through the debris, clamshells and plastic bags, praying to her new saint that the roving pack of dogs will not attack her, nor the fishermen, who watch dispassionately from boats, weaving nets of bright green acrylic.

In the house—no tapwater, no windowglass, no easy-chair—she leans against the stove and ties a sock around the wound. On the burner rests a notebook, the entries of former guests, their gratitude for a place to overindulge: sun, drink, sex. She feels excluded by their exclamation marks; she tries to imagine what she might write, tomorrow, what someone like her might have to say after the night ahead.

Outside, the setting sun begins its furor. A trail of red hearts points the way to her. Wild dogs howl.

Last Supper in the Cabinet Mountains

David Bottoms

His father-in-law read a few verses from Matthew, then, with an awkward solemnity, broke the crackers into thumbnails and passed the plate, poured the grape juice into the pill cups his wife, a nurse, had rummaged from the clinic. A big cloud was dragging a curtain of rain through the pass, already it had smudged half of the picture window gray. He leaned back into the sheepskin on the La-Z-Boy. A new family meant a new life, but starting fresh also meant a lot to learn. He watched his mother-in-law eat and drink. His wife and her sister ate and drank.

The cracker was a saltine. He raised the cup and glanced at his palm, the tangle of veins along his wrist. A minute dripped into an empty pan, and a guinea screeched from the barn. Prayer broke out on the sofa, and suddenly he understood how a wound could bleed for centuries, could trickle enough to fill these cups.

Years ago, after his divorce, he'd looked for his own way of giving up the world. He'd sat down in his kitchen and scratched a list on a grocery bag, everything he'd ever wanted, then carried it into the grove, wadded the bag, and buried it. But that was Florida, heat and booze and fever, so what could he really say had left him, and the wind had knocked him down. He'd sprawled for a long time across that grave, clutching the wet grass, while the oranges flew through the trees.

Strongman

Wendy White-Ring

He can't sleep. He flicks on the reading lamp, lifts the telephone book from the bedside table, takes two deep breaths, and rips the directory lengthwise with three quick jerks. Like yanking the drumsticks off a turkey. "Order a glass of milk," I tell him.

Instead, he puts on silver oven mitts, picks up a deck of cards, still in the box, and tears them in half. He breathes in short bursts, as if he's revving a motorcycle's engine.

At home when he's restless, he does arm curls using our golden retriever. Then, with a rope, he drags the van, loaded with our kids, up and down the dark street until sweat softens his muscles the way coarse grass turns limp with dew.

In this hotel we are two time zones away from our house. So when he asks, "Just a set," rubbing his arms that are as big around as my thighs, I say OK because even his nose looks wild.

I lie on the floor, my arms straight by my ears. He grabs my wrists and ankles, stands upright, and lifts me to his shoulders. When he pushes me over his head, I see the shape of Florida in an acoustical ceiling tile. "One," I count.

In the morning, housewives from coast to coast will watch The Magnificent Mighty Muscle, who, using only his longest finger, will balance a famous television talk show host above his head. Yet for now he is simply a man whose hands tremble not from my weight but from all that he cannot clean and jerk.

Diverging Paths and All That

Maryanne O'Hara

In Dollar Saver, the aisles are empty, customers crowding Electronics watching Nixon resign on twenty TV sets. Dad dropped us off with three bucks to buy burgers but we've already spent it on fireballs and fudge.

While Nixon keeps the manager occupied, Billy demonstrates the "heads-up technique," the nonchalant gaze, his left hand filching Hershey bars and Bic pens while his right hand jingles pocket change. Billy grins, "I really save my dollars here."

Solo time. I head for Cosmetics, the wall of Peeper Sticks—blue and green and lavender eye crayons that've always cost dollars I don't have. My hand closes around Seafoam Green, hesitates, but what the hell, even the President's a crook, so I slip it up my sleeve. I try to sneak away natural as Billy, but my legs move too quick and stiff.

Billy meets me in Electronics, where Nixon's keeping his head up, not admitting a damn thing. Saying he'd be able to clear his name if he fought long enough, but he'll sacrifice his honor for the country. When he says he'll resign as of noon the next day, I check out all these adults who yelled, "Impeach the crook." Nobody cheers. The faces are solemn as gravestones. Billy's motioning, Come on let's go, but I suddenly feel like I ate too much candy. I shake my sleeve, dropping the Peeper Stick onto a shelf, and follow Billy out the automatic doors. Dad's picking us up in two minutes, but Billy's headed someplace else.

A Gentleman's C

Padgett Powell

My father, trying to finally graduate from college at sixty-two, came, by curious circumstance, to be enrolled in an English class I taught, and I was, perhaps, a bit tougher on him than I was on the others. Hadn't he been tougher on me than on other people's kids growing up? I gave him a hard, honest, low C. About what I felt he'd always given me.

We had a death in the family, and my mother and I traveled to the funeral. My father stayed put to complete his exams—it was his final term. On the way home we learned that he had received his grades, which were low enough in the aggregate to prevent him from graduating, and reading this news on the dowdy sofa inside the front door, he leaned over as if to rest and had a heart attack and died.

For years I had thought the old man's passing away would not affect me, but it did.

Of Exposure

John Holman

His silver car, windows tight, and the sky ocean green. A layer of yellow behind that, he senses. Power lines black along the interstate looping in the wind. His exit blank, rain like a wet, cloudy mirror up ahead. He is afraid of the trees in the neighborhoods.

On the seat beside him, an electric rubber tongue. He has ordered it from a blue magazine; it arrived today at his office. He touches the box, brown. He thinks of his colleagues in the meeting, which abruptly adjourned because of the twisters. Minutes before the secretary gave the call to scram, many of them turned red. First, the man who knows where all the money comes from—red as meat. Then the computer geek, Ms. Internet—tomato. Then the new girl—night-red satin sheets, shiny boots. Then the old guy, of leather books—dusty devil tail. Some stayed white, and two pulsed pink; then a pink one went strawberry, unshaven.

Car phone, trill, but he doesn't answer. Does lightning enter cellular trails? His boys, looking out the schoolhouse window at the yellow-green sky, at the sheets of thick-fogged mirror falling. He slips off the interstate, barely seeing, and goes into the whirling trees. Daddy's coming, he signals, thinking of his wife, imagining the tongue in the box lolling in mute, microchip sensitivity, moisture activated.

They know something, the people at work, his wife and kids, the silver balls popping from the sky.

Tea Leaves

Janet Burroway

He came from Harris and Wynton to put the new program on her pc. He was thin as a digit. His fingers on the keyboard had an octave span.

Shift Search, he said, Alt F3, Control, Enter.

The CEO had circulated an austerity memo on air-conditioning, and the sweat beaded out from under her bra. The name of her new nail lacquer was Rosy Refrain; it occurred to her that this was clever without exactly making sense.

Hit the Escape key. Look, all you have to do is this and this.

You go so fast, she said. Would you like some coffee?

He eyed her briefly. I don't drink coffee.

Tea?

What kind of tea?

There was Irish Breakfast in the lounge, she thought, and maybe Camomile. The hair at her nape was curling in the damp. She herself had brought the Lemon Zinger, she pointed out. This was a judicious guess.

I don't like it too strong, he said.

I can use one tea bag for both.

When she was halfway there he called, No sugar!

She brought the tea on a copper tray, which was the best she found in the kitchenette. There were chocolate mint Girl Scout cookies from Lily Ellis's daughter's troop.

He was into the Autoexec.bat, doing something complicated as Prokofiev.

I'm afraid your tea will get cold, she said. Please drink it. Please.

He didn't look up. Once I get the program set up it practically runs by itself, he said.

We Eat Our Peas for the Souls in Purgatory

Annette McPeters

Rob laid some gum on the counter. Mr. Freed asked was that all, and Rob's voice vanished. As Mr. Freed reached over and pulled the candy bars from Rob's jacket pocket, Rob's legs ached to run, like the boy in his nightmares who flailed in a choking sea.

"You think your father needs more trouble?"

Mr. Freed's words pumped along Rob's limbs as he passed the schoolyard. Sister Therese was sweeping leaves. Rob bent his face to the asphalt. He didn't want to think about the nuns coming to pick him up, with their lies about starting diets tomorrow. He didn't want to sit jammed between them again, their haunches seeping from somber habits to the crevice of the car seat as they drove to Pelham, D'Angelo's, for pizza they couldn't resist from the bar they wouldn't enter.

The nuns never waited to eat. Yeasty fog filled the wagon; their cheeks bulged as they blessed Rob goodbye.

Down at the water he walked a rock jetty out over the Sound. The nuns said his mother was in heaven, another lie. Across the Sound, a stone angel spread her arms before miles of mown slopes. Rob's mother had accepted the angel's invitation.

The masts of moored boats chimed, off-key, as dusk came on. Rob took the other candy bars from his rear pocket, threw them on the water. Some dark flavor filled his mouth, regardless.

Waiting

Peggy McNally

Five days a week the lowest-paid substitute teacher in the district drives her father's used Mercury to Hough and 79th, where she eases it, mud flaps and all, down the ramp into the garage of Patrick Henry Junior High, a school where she'll teach back-to-back classes without so much as a coffee break and all of this depressing her until she remembers her date last night, and hopes it might lead to bigger things, maybe love, so she quickens her pace towards the main office to pick up her class lists with the names of students she'll never know as well as she has come to know the specials in the cafeteria, where she hopes the coffee will be perking and someone will have brought in those doughnuts she's come to love so much, loves more than the idea of teaching seventh-graders the meaning of a poem, because after all she's a sub who'll finish her day, head south to her father's house, and at dinner, he'll ask her how her job is going, and she'll say okay, and he'll remind her that it might lead to a full-time position with benefits but she knows what teaching in that school is like, and her date from last night calls to ask if she's busy and she says yes because she's promised her father she'd wash his car and promises to her father are sacred since her mother died, besides it's the least she can do now that he lets her drive his car five days a week towards the big lake, to the NE corner of Hough and 79th and you know the rest.

But What Was Her Name?

Dawn Raffel

She was born in December in Baraboo or thereabouts—small, still blue, a girl, and, by some trick of oxygen, alive. She lived to marry late. She bore live descendants.

See her in the pantry, a knife in the hand, a mother of sons, a baster of ribs, of scraps. There is a knot at the throat. There is a vision of something.

The groom wears wool.

The bride grows thick.

She holds her breath.

Years pass.

She is ripping a lining, draining a steampot, simmering blood. She is sinew and elbow, gnarled in a chair. Her feet are red. A man she has raised delivers a slipper. Look at him! he wear the groom's robe.

Her fingerbone will not release the ring.

"Father?" she says.

She sees her breath.

She was white in the bed of her birth. The past had taken hold of her—the heart's last sleight.

Guadalupe in the Promised Land

Sam Shepard

Guadalupe hit the skids and fishtailed into a ditch, crawled out of the wreck bleeding from the neck, saw the moon, laid his head in a mud puddle, said "Todo el Mundo" three times and snuffed out. Him and Manolete got together after that and Manolete told him it wasn't enough just to be a man. The thing was to shoot for sainthood. He said he almost hit it. A saint of the cape. Jackson Pollock joined them and told Manolete he was full of shit. A man was good enough. That was harder than sainthood. There's too many saints anyway. Guadalupe didn't know what to think. He ran into Jimmy Dean and Jimmy just looked confused. Marilyn Monroe had no opinion. Brecht kept talking about Germany and shame. Satchmo kept wiping his sweat and shuffling. Janis wanted more. Crazy Horse said: "Fight and die young." Brian Jones just played the harpoon. Dylan Thomas said "Rage." Jimi Hendrix said "Slide." Big Bopper said "What?" Johnny Ace said "Shoot." And Davey Moore said "Take it all on." That made sense to Guadalupe. And with that he lay down for a nice long rest.

Morning News

Jerome Stern

get bad news in the morning and faint. Lying on tile, I think about death and see the tombstone my wife and I saw twenty years ago in the hilly colonial cemetery in North Carolina: *Peace at last.* I wonder, where is fear? The doctor, embarrassed, picks me up off the floor and I stagger to my car. What do people do next?

I pick up my wife. I look at my wife. I think how much harder it would be for me if she were this sick. I remember the folk tale that once seemed so strange to me, of the peasant wife beating her dying husband for abandoning her. For years, people have speculated on what they would do if they only had a week, a month a year to live. Feast or fast? I feel a failure of imagination. I should want something fantastic—a final meal atop the Eiffel Tower. Maybe I missed something not being brought up in a religion that would haunt me now with an operatic final confrontation between good and evil— I try to imagine myself a Puritan fearful of damnation, a saint awaiting glory.

But I have never been able to take seriously my earnestly mystical students, their belief that they were heading to join the ringing of the eternal spheres. So my wife and I drive to the giant discount warehouse. We sit on the floor like children and, in five minutes, pick out a 60-inch television, the largest set in the whole God damn store.

Molibi

Leigh Hancock

1987 WINNER

There is not a spare inch of flesh to Molibi. She presses leather palms into my own, murmuring, "Miss Allen, Miss Allen." All elbows and knees and teeth when she dances, Molibi crooks one arm over her head and wraps her feet around the desk-chair when she sits for an exam. Her cheeks are tight drumheads, and her neck as scrawny as the sugarcane she gnaws. Only her eyes and lips are soft, abundant, wet.

Quentin, my British colleague, says Americans are

heavy on the hips and adjectives. He kindly excludes me from both judgments, but with Molibi I fall from grace. I want to describe her in flowing sentences, to pad her with adjectives, to protect her against an inevitable life of maize-stamping and childlugging. I want to convince her that she needn't haul water all her days, nor follow boys out to that narrow strip they call the Metsi-ma-sweu, Once-a-River. These things demand wide hips and square shoulders, a jaw that can clench and a soul that dog-shakes disappointments like water. Molibi has none of these and I worry for her and the place she must find in her country.

Although—Quentin assures me—I shouldn't. The boys, all knees and loose shoes themselves, don't care for the delicate girls, the fine bones and weedy waists. Such etched beauty is lost in the tangle of bony acacia on this desert plain. The boys want to drive themselves into flesh as pliant and welcoming as old, rotting wood. They choose workhorses, sofas and readily furrowed fields as their life's loves.

For a while—Quentin promises and his lips gleam—Molibi is safe.

Wallet

Allen Woodman

Tired of losing his wallet to pickpockets, my father, at seventy, makes a phony one. He stuffs the phony wallet with expired food coupons and losing Florida Lottery tickets and a fortune cookie fortune that reads, "Life is the same old story told over and over."

In a full-length mirror, he tries the wallet in the back pocket of his pants. It hangs out fat with desire. "All oyster," he says to me, "no pearl."

We drive to the mall where he says he lost the last

one. I am the wheelman, left behind in the car, while my father cases a department store.

He is an old man trying to act feeble and childlike, and he overdoes it like stage makeup on a community-theater actor. He has even brought a walking stick for special effect. Packages of stretch socks clumsily slip from his fingers. He bends over farther than he has bent in years to retrieve them, allowing the false billfold to rise like a dark wish and be grappled by the passing shadow of a hand.

Then the unexpected happens. The thief is chased by an attentive salesclerk. Others join in. The thief subdued, the clerk holds up the reclaimed item. "Your wallet, sir. Your wallet." As she begins opening it, searching for identification, my father runs toward an exit. The worthless articles float to the floor.

Now my father is in the car, shouting for me to drive away. There will be time enough for silence and rest. We are both stupid with smiles and he is shouting, "Drive fast, drive fast."

Biographical Notes

Kim Addonizio is the author of a collection of poems, *The Philosopher's Club*. Her fiction has appeared in *Chelsea* and elsewhere. She lives in San Francisco.

Roberta Allen is the author of a collection of short short stories, *The Daughter*; a novella-in-short-short-stories, *Amazon Dreams*; and *Fast Fiction*, a book on writing and the short short. She teaches short shorts at The New School, New York University, and The Writer's Voice.

Joanne Avallon teaches literature and composition at Endicott College and lives near Boston. She is a graduate of the Emerson College M.F.A. program.

Laurie Berry was the winner of the 1989 World's Best Short Short Story Contest. Her work has appeared in *Gulf Coast*, *Sundog*, and the text, *Writing Fiction*. She teaches at Miami–Dade Community College.

David Bottoms was the winner of the Walt Whitman Award for his first book of poems, *Shooting Rats at the Bibb County Dump*. He is the author of three other books of poems and two novels. He teaches at Georgia State University.

Linda Brewer was a finalist in the World's Best Short Short Story Contest.

Janet Burroway is the author of the widely used text, *Writing Fiction*, as well as plays, poetry, children's books, and seven novels, including *Raw Silk* and *Cutting Stone*. She is the Robert O. Lawton Distinguished Professor at Florida State University.

François Camoin was the winner of the 1991 World's Best Short Short Story Contest. He is the author of *The End of the World Is Los Angeles* and *Why Men Are Afraid of Women*. He teaches at the University of Utah.

Ron Carlson is the author of two story collections, *The News of the World* and *Plan B for the Middle Class*, and two novels, *Betrayed by F. Scott Fitzgerald* and *Truants*. He teaches at Arizona State University.

Fred Chappell is the author of numerous books, including the novel *More Shapes Than One* and *Sources: Poems.* Selected works are available in *The Fred Chappell Reader.* He teaches at the University of North Carolina at Greensboro.

Marilyn Chin's books of poetry include *The Phoenix Gone, The Terrace Empty,* and *Dwarf Bamboo.* She teaches creative writing at San Diego State University.

Judith Ortiz Cofer is the author of a story collection, *An Island Like You: Stories of the Barrio,* and a novel, *The Line of the Sun,* as well as *The Latin Deli: Prose and Poetry.* She teaches at Georgia State University.

Rick DeMarinis is the author of a story collection and two novels, *The Year of the Zinc Penny* and *The Mortician's Apprentice.* He teaches at the University of Texas–El Paso.

Stephen Dunning was the winner of the 1990 World's Best Short Short Story Contest. He is the author of two story collections, including *Hunter's Park and Other Stories.* He lives in Ann Arbor.

Stuart Dybek's short shorts and prose poems appear in two books, *Brass Knuckles* and *The Coast of Chicago.* He teaches at Western Michigan University.

Russell Edson is the author of numerous books including *The Reason Why the Closet-Man is Never Sad*, *The Song of Percival Peacock*, and *The Tunnel: Selected Poems*.

Roberto Fernandez is the author of two novels, *Raining Backwards* and *Holy Radishes!* He teaches in the modern languages department at Florida State University.

Tom Fleming was the winner of the 1995 World's Best Short Short Story Contest. A native of Arizona, he now lives outside Chicago, where he is working on a novel based on the life of Harry Houdini.

George Garrett has written over twenty-five books—fiction, poetry, essays—including the justly celebrated Elizabethan Trilogy. He is Henry Hoyns professor of English at the University of Virginia in Charlottesville.

Molly Giles is the author of *Rough Translations*. She teaches creative writing at San Francisco State University.

Jamie Granger was the winner of the 1994 World's Best Short Short Story Contest. He grew up on Montserrat, in the West Indies, and currently lives in Montgomery, Alabama.

Leigh Hancock was the winner of the 1987 World's Best Short Short Story Contest.

Ursula Hegi is the author of a collection of stories and four novels, including *Salt Dancers* and *Stones from the River*. She teaches creative writing at Eastern Washington University.

Amy Hempel is the author of two story collections, *Reasons to Live* and *At the Gates of the Animal Kingdom*. She also coedited *Unleashed: Poems by Writers' Dogs*. She lives in New York City.

John Holman is the author of the collection *Squabble and Other Stories*. He teaches at Georgia State University in Atlanta.

Harry Humes was the winner of the 1993 World's Best Short Short Story Contest. He is the author of three books of poetry, including *The Way Winter Works* and *The Bottomland*, and is the founding editor of the poetry journal *Yarrow*. He lives in Pennsylvania.

James Kelman is the author of *The Burn*, *A Chancer*, and *How Late It Was, How Late*, for which he received the Booker Prize.

Betsy Kemper is working on an M.F.A. at Emerson College. Her fiction has appeared in the *North American Review*. She lives in Boston.

Jesse Lee Kercheval is the author of a novel, *The Museum of Happiness*, and a collection of stories, *The Dogeater*, which won the Associated Writing Programs Award in Short Fiction. She lives in Madison, Wisconsin.

Mariette Lippo was a finalist in the World's Best Short Short Story Contest.

Monifa A. Love is a graduate student in creative writing at Florida State University. Her work has appeared in *American Voice*, *New Letters*, and the *African American Review*. She lives in Tallahassee.

Elaine Magarrell is the author of two books of poems, *On Hogback Mountain* and *Blameless Lives*. She works for the District of Columbia as a writer in residence in the public schools.

Michael Martone is the author of four story collections, including *Alive and Dead in Indiana*, *Safety Patrol*, and *Seeing Eye*. He teaches creative writing at Syracuse University.

Beauvais McCaddon grew up in Mississippi and now lives in Florida. She is a graduate of the Florida State University writing program. Her stories have appeared in the *Virginia Quarterly* and *Quarterly West*.

Michael McFee has published five books of poetry, including *Colander*, and edited the anthology *The Language They Speak Is Things to Eat: Poems by Fifteen Contemporary North Carolina Poets*. He teaches creative writing at the University of North Carolina at Chapel Hill.

Peggy McNally is Dean of Admissions of the law school at Cleveland State University and a graduate of the Vermont College M.F.A. program. She lives in Cleveland Heights, Ohio.

Annette McPeters was the winner of the 1988 World's Best Short Short Story Contest.

E. Ethelbert Miller is the author of *Seasons of Hunger, Cry of Rain: Poems 1975–1990* as well as editor of *In Search of Color Everywhere: A Collection of African American Poetry*. He teaches at Howard University.

Antonya Nelson is the author of a novel and three story collections, *The Expendables*, *In the Land of Men*, and *Family Terrorists*. She teaches creative writing at New Mexico State University and for the Warren Wilson M.F.A. program.

Maryanne O'Hara is a graduate of the writing program at Emerson College. She lives in Ashland, Massachusetts.

Pamela Painter is the author of a story collection, *Getting to Know the Weather*, and coauthor of *What If? Writing Exercises for Fiction Writers*. She is Writer in Residence at Emerson College and teaches in the Vermont College M.F.A. program.

Padgett Powell is the author of *Edisto* and *A Woman Called Drown*. He teaches creative writing at the University of Florida.

Dawn Raffel is the author of the short story collection, *In The Year of Long Division*. She is the fiction editor of *Redbook*.

Sam Shepard is the author of many plays, including *True West*, *Fool for Love*, and *Buried Child* for which he won the Pulitzer Prize.

Robert Shuster was a finalist in the World's Best Short Short Story Contest. His stories have appeared in the *Alaska Quarterly Review* and *Yellow Silk*. He lives in Seattle.

Natalia Rachel Singer was the winner of the 1992 World's Best Short Short Story Contest and was a finalist several times as well. She teaches at St. Lawrence University.

Jerome Stern is the author of *Making Shapely Fiction*, a commentator for National Public Radio, and the originator of The World's Best Short Short Story competition. He directs the creative writing program at Florida State University.

Virgil Suarez was born in Cuba. He is the author of a story collection and three novels, including *Havana Thursdays*. He also coedited *Iguana Dreams: New Latino Fiction* and *Paper Dance: 55 Latino Poets*. He teaches creative writing and literature at Florida State University.

Ron Wallace is the author of nine books, including *Time's Fancy* and *The Makings of Happiness*. He is the director of the creative writing program at the University of Wisconsin and divides his time between Madison and a forty-acre farm in Bear Valley, Wisconsin.

Linda Wendling grew up in Wyoming but now lives in St. Louis, where she owns a consulting firm and also teaches at the University of Missouri, St. Louis.

Wendy White-Ring has published stories in the *North American Review*, the *American Literary Review*, and the *Southeast Review*. She is a creative writing instructor at Phoenix College.

Joy Williams is the author of *Escapes*, *Taking Care*, *Breaking and Entering*, and *The Florida Keys: A History and Guide*. She lives in Florida.

Allen Woodman is the author of *The Shoebox of Desire and Other Stories* and *All-You-Can-Eat, Alabama*, as well as several children's books. He directs the creative writing program at Northern Arizona University.

Permissions